BEING BRAVE

Written by Angela Kecojevic

Illustrated by Maribel Lechuga

OXFORD
UNIVERSITY PRESS

Brave narrowed her eyes and observed the tundra.

Black rocks peeked through the snow and cities of ice were beginning to thaw. It was winter in the Arctic circle, but Brave's playground was already melting, the way it usually did in spring.

The snow fox sniffed the air. She smelled the rich scents of bearberries and lemmings. But there was something else in the air that she didn't recognize. Perhaps it was the strange trees her mother had told her about.

'The ground is softer on the higher slopes, and trees are appearing for the first time,' said her mother as they prepared for their evening hunt. 'Our cousins, the red foxes, have also been hunting here.'

Brave's sisters, Swift and Tag, scampered out into the snow, eager to hunt.

'May I stay at home and guard the den?' Brave asked.

Mother nuzzled Brave's fur. 'Yes, but be as brave as your name, little one. We will be back home soon enough.'

'Before the stars go away?' Brave asked, trying not to sound too hopeful.

'Before you get too hungry!' Mother growled playfully.

Brave was given her name at the first fall
of snow, like all snow fox cubs. As magical
as the frozen landscape looked, it could be
deadly to a young and inexperienced cub.

Her father said she would grow into her name.
She must find out how to be Brave.

'But what if I don't,' Brave whispered to herself as she watched her family fade into the distance.

'What if I never find my brave?'

She crept back into the den, feeling small and alone.

During the summer, when her coat was earthy brown and the scent of wild cotton grass sweetened the air, Brave felt happy and safe.

But as winter approached, and her fur grew long and white, Brave watched her world changing.

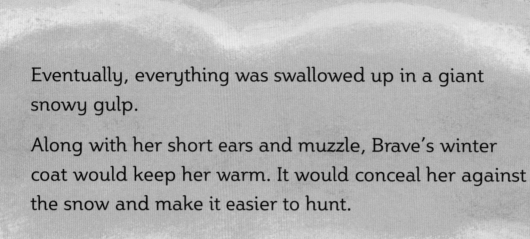

Eventually, everything was swallowed up in a giant snowy gulp.

Along with her short ears and muzzle, Brave's winter coat would keep her warm. It would conceal her against the snow and make it easier to hunt.

But what if the snow swallowed her too, and she became lost?

That's what scared her the most.

Father said that one day the snow might
vanish forever. If that happened, they
might need to find a new home.

But Brave couldn't imagine living anywhere else.
The tundra was her home.

With her tail tucked around her for warmth,

Brave watched the snowflakes pirouette

and dance with the wind.

One snowflake fluttered on to
her nose, an intricate white pattern.
Brave snapped at it playfully,
edging out into the snow.

13

She danced with the snowflakes, jumping and then falling, as though catching tasty lemmings.

Pounce, pounce.
Pounce, pounce.

Brave only stopped playing when she realized she could no longer see her den. The wind was whipping snow into the air, creating a cyclone of white.

She no longer knew which way was home.

In the distance, Brave spied a row of snow-covered trees where she could shelter. But to reach them would mean crossing the tundra alone.

There might be hunters.

Predators.

She would need to stay alert.

Yet it was the Arctic wind that became her real enemy, harsh and strong in its attack. Brave lowered her head and fought back.

Brave reached the treeline, weary and hungry. As she crept over a fine layer of snow, she caught the smell of the trees, sweet and sharp. Her eyes drifted shut and she dreamt of the stars that would guide her safely home.

drip

drip

drip

Brave thought the stars in her dream were melting, until she awoke and realized that icy drops of water were *falling* from the tree.

She tilted her head as the sound of the river reached her ears.

'Bearberries, bearberries, bearberries,' it seemed to sing.

Brave licked her lips, picturing the juicy red berries.
It had been hours since she'd last eaten.

Brave weaved her way around **jagged rocks** and padded over thawing ice until she reached the river.

The water levels were high for this time of the year, and they made her heart flutter.

She spotted a bearberry bush lower down on the riverbank, the berries unexpectedly plump. Despite the thick fur on her paws which helped her to walk on snow and ice, she proceeded carefully.

Swoosh!

A snowy owl swooped towards her, dusting her head with its great white wings.

Brave charged along the riverbank, desperate to escape. She was used to running on snow, so this softer ground, hidden beneath ice and water, made it difficult. As the owl's sharp claws skimmed her back, she lost her footing and tumbled into the icy river below.

22

Brave had only swum in gentle waters before, and she struggled to keep her head above the current. Chunks of broken ice surrounded her and the song of the river became a tuneless roar.

Mother's words echoed in her head.

'Be as brave as your name, little one.'

'I'm trying to be brave,' she whispered.
'I'm trying.'

Brave spotted a patch of shrubs and Arctic willows hanging over the river. She swam towards them.

Using her claws and teeth to help, Brave clambered onto the slopes of the riverbank.

The scent of other animals tickled her nose, and she stayed hidden in the snow.

She wasn't safe yet. In the distance beyond, polar bears would be out hunting and there might be other predators roaming the tundra.

With the fur on her paws muffling her movements, Brave padded quickly and quietly across the tundra.

'It's time to go home,' she whispered to the stars.

Now, she understood what her father had meant.
Being brave was something she needed to find.

Brave ran into the night, guided
by the stars. A white hare darted
across her path and somewhere in the
distance she heard the chilling howl of
a wolf. She stopped and sniffed the air.
It was close.

Brave carried on running, no longer afraid, towards the star
that shone brightly above her home: the North star, *Polaris*.

Now that the snow had stopped falling, the tundra
smelled sweeter, the way it did in summer.

Two shapes appeared on the horizon, accompanied by a soft yowling sound. It was her mother and father! Brave yowled back. They had come to find her.

Back in her den, snuggled up to her sisters,
Brave talked about her adventure.

'The ultimate adventure,' she murmured sleepily.
'*Where I found my brave.*'

As the Arctic animals slept, their frozen world was slowly changing and they might soon have new dangers to face.

They would all need their brave.

OXFORD
UNIVERSITY PRESS

Great Clarendon Street, Oxford, OX2 6DP, United Kingdom

Oxford University Press is a department of the University of Oxford. It furthers the University's objective of excellence in research, scholarship, and education by publishing worldwide. Oxford is a registered trade mark of Oxford University Press in the UK and in certain other countries

Text © Oxford University Press 2023

Illustrations © Maribel Lechuga 2023

The moral rights of the author have been asserted

First published 2023

British Library Cataloguing in Publication Data

Data available

ISBN:978-1-382-04079-2

The manufacturing process conforms to the environmental regulations of the country of origin.

Printed in the UK by Bell and Bain Ltd, Glasgow

Acknowledgements

Series Editor: James Clements

Written by Angela Kecojevic

Illustrated by Maribel Lechuga

Author photo courtesy of Angela Kecojevic

Every effort has been made to contact copyright holders of material reproduced in this book. Any omissions will be rectified in subsequent printings if notice is given to the publisher.

MIX
Paper | Supporting responsible forestry
FSC® C007785
www.fsc.org